But It's True!

Written by Heather Gemmen
Illustrated by Luciano Lagares

Equipping Kids for Life!

Faith Parenting Guide

Ages 4-7 Truth

A Faith Parenting Guide can be found on page 32.

"Where were you, Jon?" my daddy asked
when I came running in.
"I was fighting giant frogs!"
I saw my daddy grin.

"Great big frogs in our back yard?"
My daddy laughed out loud.

"It must be tough to fight such things.
You make me very proud."

"Great big frogs and tiny cows—
they're all behind the shed.

I had to save the little guys
and send the frogs to bed.

"I'm sure you must have also seen the purple flying cats,

the talking pigs, the laughing ducks,
and yellow-bellied rats.

"I saw them all!" I told my dad.
This game was fun to play.
"I also saw a horse that danced.
He said to me, 'Good day.'"

My daddy pulled me in his arms.
"Your imagination's great!
I'm glad God gave this gift to you
at the perfect age of eight."

"But, Dad, my teacher sometimes says
these stories can't be told.
She always likes to say to me,
'Jon, truth is good as gold.'"

"She's right, you know," my daddy said.
"It says so in the Word:
'Do not lie' can't be more clear.
Your teacher's not absurd."

"But, Dad, you surely can't believe
in yellow-bellied rats!
Don't you know that all this time
there've been no flying cats?"

"I know there are no tiny cows.
I know that these are games.
I also know when you deny
you've called your brother names.

"God loves imagination—
a creative type himself.

He just can't stand to see such gifts
get put upon a shelf."

I ran to grab my markers
so God would not be mad.

"You shouldn't tell a single lie,
but stories make me glad."

"Where were you, Jon?" my teacher asked when I was running late.

"I was hiding from a great big troll!
It got out of its crate."

My teacher kind of looked at me.
I knew that I was wrong.
"That's a tale," I quickly said.
"The truth: I took too long."

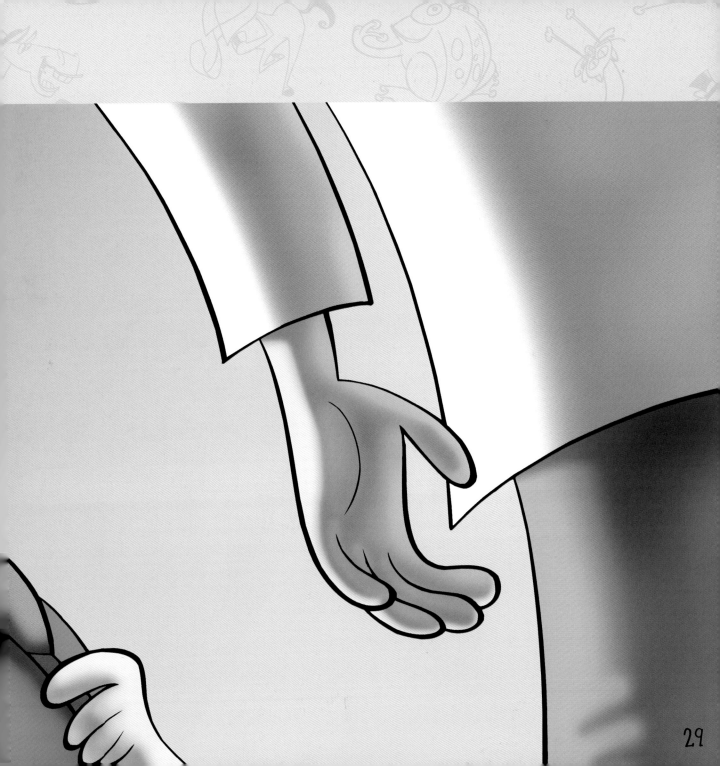

"Well, write your funny story down and draw a picture, too.

We'll take it to a contest.
You just might win a blue."

But It's True!

Life Issue: I want my children to stop lying.

Spiritual Building Block: Truth

Do the following activities to help your children balance truth and imagination:

 Sight: Ask your children to tell you what their house looks like. Explain the only way they can answer you is with a drawing.

Compare their finished picture with your actual house. Make sure it is the same color, has a door in the same place as yours, and has the same shaped roof. Check to see if the drawing is telling the truth to somebody's question, "What does your house look like?"

Next have them draw a picture of a house one of their stuffed animals or dolls might live in. Explain that this drawing is make-believe. It could be any color or shape. It could have a doorbell on the chimney or a slide coming out the windows.

Tell your children God is pleased they can tell the truth when asked what their home looks like, and he is excited about your children's creativity when they imagine a home for their snuggle friend.

But It's True!

Life Issue: I want my children to stop lying.

Spiritual Building Block: Truth

Do the following activities to help your children balance truth and imagination:

Sound: Make a tape recording for your children of some familiar sounds—a dog barking, the microwave beeping, the lawnmower buzzing, or anything else your children will readily recognize.

Have them listen to the tape of the real noises and creatively act out the sounds with them. You could get on all fours and bark like a puppy, push pretend buttons in the air to cook an imaginary meal, and hold out your arms in front of you as you walk around the room as if cutting the grass.

Explain that the sound on the tape is real, and what you are doing with them is make-believe. Both have a place in God's world. It isn't lying to pretend. It is lying when someone asks you for the truth and you give a pretend answer.

But It's True!

Life Issue: I want my children to stop lying.

Spiritual Building Block: Truth

Do the following activities to help your children balance truth and imagination:

 Touch: Blindfold your children or, if they don't feel comfortable with a blindfold, have them close their eyes.

Describe to them an object and then have them touch it to determine if you are telling the truth or making up a funny story.

If they think you are telling the truth they say, "Truth." If they think you are pretending they say, "Pretend."

For example, take your kids into the kitchen and say, "I have a fuzzy peach the size of a baseball", and then place a peach in their hands. They will be able to identify the soft surface, shape, and size as that of a peach, and they'll say, "Truth."

Say, "I have a big, smooth, round watermelon", and then place a sponge in their hands. You can both immediately giggle at the silliness of your description as they try to say, "Pretend", through their laughter.

Get all of These Great Tough Stuff Titles for Your Child!

Heather Gemmen

Growing up can be a hard thing. That's why we created the Tough Stuff for Kids Series! The delightful art and pleasant rhyme of these books make reading these stories enjoyable for young children. They will want to read the stories over and over again while parents will love the spiritual lessons and help for the Tough Stuff kids face.

8 x 8   Paperback   36P each

0-78144-036-X

0-78144-034-3

0-78144-035-1

0-78143-853-5

0-78143-851-9

0-78143-852-7

0-78143-854-3

Order Your Copies Today!
Order Online: www.cookministries.com
Phone: 1-800-323-7543
Or Visit your Local Christian Bookstore

The Word at Work Around the World

What would you do if you wanted to share God's love with children on the streets of your city? That's the dilemma David C. Cook faced in 1870's Chicago. His answer was to create literature that would capture children's hearts.

Out of those humble beginnings grew a worldwide ministry that has used literature to proclaim God's love and disciple generation after generation. Cook Communications Ministries is committed to personal discipleship—to helping people of all ages learn God's Word, embrace his salvation, walk in his ways, and minister in his name.

Faith Kidz, RiverOak, Honor, Life Journey, Victor, NextGen . . . every time you purchase a book produced by Cook Communications Ministries, you not only meet a vital personal need in your life or in the life of someone you love, but you're also a part of ministering to José in Colombia, Humberto in Chile, Gousa in India, or Lidiane in Brazil. You help make it possible for a pastor in China, a child in Peru, or a mother in West Africa to enjoy a life-changing book. And because you helped, children and adults around the world are learning God's Word and walking in his ways.

Thank you for your partnership in helping to disciple the world. May God bless you with the power of his Word in your life.

For more information about our international ministries,
visit www.ccmi.org.